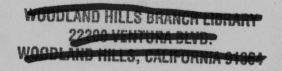
WOODLAND HILLS BRANCH LIBRARY
22200 VENTURA BLVD.
WOODLAND HILLS, CALIFORNIA 91364

W9-CPC-129

MAXI, THE STAR

AUG 1 5 2006

MAXI, THE STAR

by Debra and Sal Barracca

pictures by Alan Ayers

▪▪▪▪▪▪▪▪▪▪▪▪▪▪▪▪▪▪▪▪▪▪

Dial Books for Young Readers
New York

X2
B
169964823

NEW YORK
AK9 2GO

Published by Dial Books for Young Readers
A Division of Penguin Books USA Inc.
375 Hudson Street, New York, New York 10014

Text copyright © 1993 by Debra and Sal Barracca
Pictures copyright © 1993 by Halcyon Books Inc.
All rights reserved
Created and designed by Halcyon Books Inc.
Printed in the U.S.A.
First Edition
1 3 5 7 9 10 8 6 4 2

Library of Congress Cataloging in Publication Data
Barracca, Debra. Maxi, the star/by Debra and Sal Barracca;
pictures by Alan Ayers.
p. cm.
Summary: Maxi and Jim take their taxi cross-country so that
Maxi can do a screen test for Doggie Bites.
ISBN 0-8037-1348-7 (trade).—ISBN 0-8037-1349-5 (lib. bdg.)
[1. Dogs—Fiction. 2. United States—Description and travel—Fiction.
3. Television advertising—Fiction. 4. Stories in rhyme.]
I. Barracca, Sal. II. Ayers, Alan, ill. III. Title.
PZ8.3.B25263Max 1993   [E]—dc20   91-44962   CIP   AC

The art for this book was prepared by using oil paints.
It was then color-separated and reproduced in red, yellow, blue, and black halftones.

To Alan Ayers, a true star.
D.B. and S.B.

To my wife Jeanne,
for her unwavering support.
A.A.

"Wake up, Jim, it's late!
       It's a quarter past eight—
              Our taxi is waiting, let's hurry!"
Jim patted my head
       As he jumped out of bed.
              "We've got plenty of time, don't you worry!"

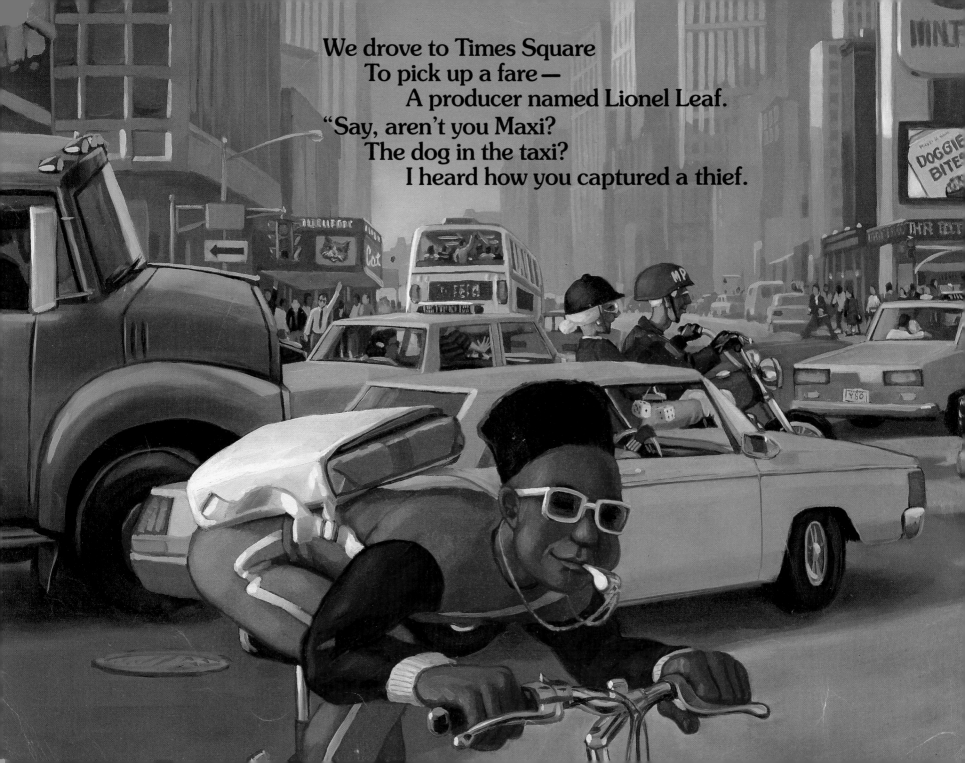

We drove to Times Square
To pick up a fare —
A producer named Lionel Leaf.
"Say, aren't you Maxi?
The dog in the taxi?
I heard how you captured a thief.

"I've been looking all over
  To find a new 'Rover'—
    At last, what good luck, here you are!
"You must come out west
  To do a screen test—
    You could be our Doggie Bites star!"

The very next day
    We took off for L.A.
        New York became smaller behind us.
We'd miss it, we knew,
    But that great city view
        Would stay in our hearts to remind us.

We headed out west,
    Then we needed to rest.
        Up ahead was a sign that flashed "EATS."
Huge trucks rumbled past
    And their horns gave a blast
        That made us jump out of our seats!

Under blue Kansas skies,
What a sight met our eyes!
Row upon row of gold wheat
That swayed in the breeze,
And in worn dungarees
There was an old farmer named Pete.

"Howdy!" he said
    As he scratched his gray head.
        "You ain't from around here, I take it?"
He leaned on the rail
    As we told him our tale.
        "Well, good luck now, I hope you folks make it!"

On to Yellowstone Park
  Before it grew dark.
    Old Faithful was starting to spout.
We watched, unaware
  That a huge grizzly bear
    Had come close and was lurking about.

We camped out that night
And had such a fright
        When we heard a loud, threatening growl.
Along came a ranger
        Who said, "There's no danger—
        We caught a big bear on the prowl!"

We packed up our load,
    And got back on the road.
        Great mountains soared up to the sky.
"They're the Rockies!" Jim said
    As I tilted my head.
        (And I thought New York buildings were high!)

We came to a stop
    And heard clippety-clop.
        A cowboy rode tall in the saddle.
He came by to chat,
    Tipped his ten-gallon hat,
        And then went back to tending his cattle.

California, at last!
  The trip went so fast.
    The "HOLLYWOOD" sign seemed to greet us.
At our first-class hotel
  We were treated so well—
    Mr. Leaf sent a limo to meet us!

We arrived at the lot,
    I was nervous and hot.
        Mr. Leaf said, "Just be who you are."
He then ran the test.
    "You're clearly the best —
        You *are* the new Doggie Bites star!"

The commercial was shot.
   "That's a wrap, thanks a lot!"
      Mr. Leaf said, "Okay, let's do lunch.
"This ad just can't miss,
   You're a natural at this—
      I'm glad that I followed my hunch."

Our trip was all done.
    It was tiring but fun.
        Back home was the best place to be,
But now it all seemed
    Like adventures we'd dreamed,
        Until…

Guess who we saw on TV?